GET A CLUE

THE TREASURE OF BLACKBIRD ROCK

A PICTURE MYSTERY

GET A CLUE

THE TREASURE OF BLACKBIRD ROCK
A PICTURE MYSTERY

Julian Press

GROSSET & DUNLAP

GROSSET & DUNLAP
Published by the Penguin Group
Penguin Group (USA) Inc., 375 Hudson Street, New York, New York 10014, USA
Penguin Group (Canada), 90 Eglinton Avenue East, Suite 700, Toronto, Ontario M4P 2Y3, Canada
(a division of Pearson Penguin Canada Inc.)
Penguin Books Ltd., 80 Strand, London WC2R 0RL, England
Penguin Group Ireland, 25 St. Stephen's Green, Dublin 2, Ireland
(a division of Penguin Books Ltd.)
Penguin Group (Australia), 250 Camberwell Road, Camberwell, Victoria 3124, Australia
(a division of Pearson Australia Group Pty. Ltd.)
Penguin Books India Pvt. Ltd., 11 Community Centre, Panchsheel Park, New Delhi—110 017, India
Penguin Group (NZ), 67 Apollo Drive, Rosedale, North Shore 0632, New Zealand
(a division of Pearson New Zealand Ltd.)
Penguin Books (South Africa) (Pty.) Ltd., 24 Sturdee Avenue,
Rosebank, Johannesburg 2196, South Africa

Penguin Books Ltd., Registered Offices: 80 Strand, London WC2R 0RL, England

Copyright © 2006 by cbj Verlag, a division of Verlagsgrupped Random House GmbH, Munchen, Germany.
Translated and adapted by the Miller Literary Agency, LLC. All rights reserved.
Cover background copyright © Mayang Murni Adnin, 2001-2006.
Published by Grosset & Dunlap in 2008, a division of Penguin Young Readers Group,
345 Hudson Street, New York, New York 10014.
GROSSET & DUNLAP is a trademark of Penguin Group (USA) Inc.
Printed in the U.S.A.

Library of Congress Control Number: 2007045311

ISBN 978-0-448-44873-2   10 9 8 7 6 5 4 3 2 1

NTRODUCTION

The Sugar Shack sold the best candy in Hillsdale, the tiny town where best friends Josh, David, and Lily lived. The Sugar Shack was owned by Lily Shipman's uncle, Frank. Lily, David, and Josh spent a lot of time there after school. Sometimes Lily's other uncle, Tony, dropped by. Tony was a police detective and a sucker for lollipops. The three friends loved mysteries, suspense stories, and solving puzzles, so they constantly harassed Tony with questions about his work. One day Tony suggested they start up their own detective agency. They could use the candy storage room in the attic of the Sugar Shack as their headquarters, and Frank and Tony could be their technical consultants. The three friends jumped at the chance! It was no time at all before they solved their very first case . . .

MEET THE DETECTIVES

 Frank Shipman, the owner of the Sugar Shack, is like some of the chocolates he sells: tough on the outside, gooey on the inside.

 Josh Rigby has eagle eyes and loves gadgets. His pockets are always full of tools to use in unexpected situations.

 Lily Shipman is extremely athletic. She's fast and competitive. She loves a good challenge.

 Inspector Tony Shipman is a computer whiz. He gave his old computer to the detectives, who sometimes use it when working on a case.

 David Doyle has a sensitive ear, especially for birdcalls. The clucking of his loyal cockatoo, Robinson, is like a second language to him.

 Robinson the cockatoo is David's sidekick. More than one criminal has gotten into a flap with Robinson's wings.

You can help Lily, David, Josh, and friends solve the mysteries in this book. Just read the stories, and try to answer the questions. Here's a hint: look at the pictures for clues!

CLUE ONE: Seven Little Blackbirds

It was a hot June morning when a group of sixth-grade students from Hillsdale Middle School left for a field trip. Their destination: the Abbey of Blackbird Rock. Lily, David, and Josh were among the students in attendance. Their social studies teacher, Mr Johnson, even let Robinson, David's cockatoo, come along.

The bus wound its way through the pine forest on the way to the abbey. David felt woozy, so he rested his head against the window. When he heard a chorus of "Oohs!" and "Aahs!" from his classmates, he quickly opened his eyes. There it was! The huge stone monastery appeared on a plateau in the distance.

The Abbey of Blackbird Rock was made of gigantic stones and its walls were covered with ivy. The deafening caws of a flock of ravens perched on top of the bell tower greeted the children as they descended from the bus. Father Anselm greeted the children and took them on a tour.

"Built from the remains of a medieval European chapel, the abbey was carried to America in pieces and rebuilt here in 1835," he began. "According to legend, seven ravens guided Brother Roger to this rock. The abbey was named for the birds, and seven of them have watched over it since its construction . . ."

"Oh no," Father Anselm interrupted himself, "I only see six!"

**QUESTION:** Where was the seventh blackbird? Josh knew where it was.

CLUE TWO: Father Anselm's Second Surprise

Father Anselm calmed down once Josh pointed out the missing blackbird. The bird was hiding behind the broom that leaned against the left tower wall.

"Silly bird," Father Anselm cried. "Go join your brothers!"

Then he guided his visitors into the majestic abbey sanctuary. Daylight streamed through the colorful stained-glass windows into the vast center aisle, reflecting red, blue, green, and gold onto the tile floor. He waited for the small group to reassemble around him before continuing his speech.

"Can you see the great stone pillars on each side of the aisle, children? Go ahead, try to put your arms around them."

The children rushed to encircle the pillars; it took no fewer than three to surround each one.

"These pillars alone," explained Father Anselm, "support the weight of the vaulted ceiling, which appears so light. Creating a vast space that defies the law of gravity required incredible ingenuity—"

He interrupted himself again, shocked. The door to the garden outside was ajar, even though access was strictly prohibited! David went over and looked out through an arched window. Father Anselm definitely had reason to worry!

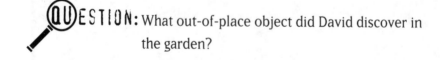

QUESTION: What out-of-place object did David discover in the garden?

CLUE THREE: The Dormitory Discovery

David saw it right away: There was a key lying at the foot of the shrub in the opposite corner of the garden. This meant that someone had gone into the garden through the abbey, despite the big sign on the front of the door announcing that access to the garden was strictly forbidden during renovations. David signaled his discovery to Lily and Josh.

When the field trip was over, Mr. Johnson and the students left—all except David, Josh, and Lily, whose research project, by happy coincidence, was on the topic of monastery herb gardens.

Father Anselm showed them the library, which contained botanical books that would be useful in writing their paper. Then the friends had lunch with the thirteen monks who still lived in the abbey. The meal passed in silence, but this didn't stop the three detectives' investigative wheels from turning. Who went into the garden? And why?

Throughout the meal, Lily had been keeping an eye on the southern wing of the abbey where the monks' sleeping quarters were located. Suddenly, she leaned in toward her friends.

"There's someone in the dormitory," she whispered.

 **QUESTION:** What made Lily so sure of the presence of an intruder?

CLUE FOUR: Midnight Mayhem

The gang told Father Anselm that they thought someone was prowling through the dormitory of the south wing. The detectives saw that the blinds of the window on the far right-hand side of the second floor had been lowered over the course of lunch. Quickly, Father Anselm took a count of the monks. All thirteen were present. Who, then, was prowling through the dormitory of the south wing?

When Father Anselm went to the dormitory to investigate, there was no one there. On the way back to lunch, he couldn't stop himself from smiling. These kids had big imaginations, but maybe they were just a little too big. He couldn't believe that he had fallen for their game! He scolded himself.

But then again, how could he explain the key in the garden? Father Anselm sighed. Maybe the brother in charge of the garden, who tended to be forgetful, had dropped his key. Father Anselm made a mental note to ask him about it later.

Father Anselm showed the three friends to a monk's cell, which would be their guest room for the night.

"We wake at dawn," said Father Anselm. "Sweet dreams, children."

The detectives tried to sleep, but they couldn't stop thinking about the mystery. As the abbey's bells chimed midnight, Lily heard voices coming from the garden. She woke the others. They dressed quickly and crept downstairs. But when they got to the garden, all was quiet. After a few minutes, the three friends were almost ready to go back to their cell when Josh pointed his finger at something moving in the shadows.

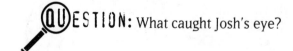

QUESTION: What caught Josh's eye?

CLUE FIVE: The Key to Success

Walking on their tiptoes, the young detectives approached the small staircase at the back of the garden. The sandals that Josh had spotted in the shadows underneath the stairs were attached to a person! It was one of the monks lying on the ground, tied up with a cord. David shook with fear as he took the monk's wrist in his trembling hands. The monk still had a pulse!

"He's alive!" David whispered. "He's just unconscious." Josh ran for help. Five minutes later, he returned with Father Anselm.

"Goodness gracious!" Father Anselm shouted as he recognized Brother Bertram, the most gentle of men. "Help me lift him, children!"

They carried Brother Bertram to the infirmary, where he started to regain consciousness. He was groaning. He tried to remember what had happened: "I was studying in the library when I heard glass breaking outside. I ran toward the square tower and saw a silhouette moving in the darkness. It was a man in a robe. He knocked me over, put his hand over my mouth, and dragged me to the ground . . ."

Brother Bertram was exhausted. While Father Anselm rubbed Brother Bertram's temples with a balm, the three friends ducked out of the room. As David headed for the door, he spied a set of keys that Father Anselm had left on the table. He discreetly slipped the keys in his pocket. They had to investigate the square tower.

The kids used the keys to inspect each room. Finally, on the third floor, they discovered something. Brother Bertram's assailant had been here!

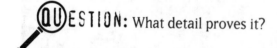 **QUESTION:** What detail proves it?

CLUE SIX: The Stranger Didn't Take the Stairs

A careful examination of the office revealed that the cord of the curtains on the window was torn off. Brother Bertram had been tied up with the missing part of the cord.

Father Anselm caught up with the kids and gasped when he entered the room. He stammered and pointed. The three friends turned to discover the source of his distress. The safe! Its door was wide open, yet it showed no signs of having been tampered with.

"This safe is where we keep our most ancient and precious liturgical objects," he explained. "David, if I may have my key ring back, please." David sheepishly returned the keys.

Father Anselm verified that the key to the room and the key to the safe were still on his keychain. How could the thief have entered the room if the door was locked?

"I've got it!" exclaimed David. "Do you see the broken glass? Whoever broke in came in through the window in the back of the room after breaking one of the panes."

"Really?" asked Josh. "And how did he break in through a window on the third floor? I don't see a ladder."

David didn't have an answer. The three friends helped Father Anselm take an inventory of the safe and then they went back to their cell. Lily opened the skylight of their room and popped her head out to look at the area surrounding the square tower.

"Come and look. I think I've found how the thief reached the third floor!" she exclaimed.

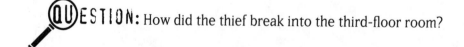 **QUESTION:** How did the thief break into the third-floor room?

CLUE SEVEN: A Needle in a Haystack

A rope was tied to the chimney of the square tower. It seemed that the thief had reached the third floor by flinging up a grappling hook, then scaling the side of the tower to the window.

"Look!" said David. He pointed to a man dressed as a monk running through the garden.

"That's definitely not Father Anselm. I can see Father Anselm in the window of the tower," said Josh. "And it isn't Brother Bertram. He's too banged up to run. Who could it be? And what is he carrying under his arm?"

"That's what we're going to find out," said Lily, rushing toward the stairs. "Come on. Hurry up or he'll get away again."

Just as Lily entered the garden, she saw the suspect head for the forest, where he vanished instantly.

"I don't know if you noticed—" Lily began.

"That he wasn't carrying anything?" interrupted David. "If only we knew where he hid whatever he was carrying."

"I know," announced Josh, rather proud of himself. "Follow me."

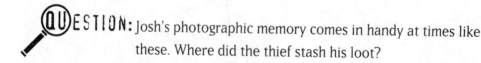

QUESTION: Josh's photographic memory comes in handy at times like these. Where did the thief stash his loot?

CLUE EIGHT: The Fruits of Their Labors

Josh ran toward the potted lemon tree in the garden. When he had seen the tree earlier from the window of the guest room, he had noticed that the lemon hanging from the tree's branch was on the right, and now it was on the left. Josh concluded that in the time it had taken the kids to reach the garden, the intruder had moved the lemon tree. But why? Josh was pretty sure he knew the answer.

"Come help me," he said. "I think we'll find a surprise."

The friends moved the lemon tree and discovered a plastic bag with a heavy object inside behind the pot. Josh plunged his hand into the bag and found a beautifully decorated silver chalice. It looked like it had to be one of the treasures that Father Anselm kept in the safe.

"But how did you know it was there?" Lily asked.

"Simple powers of deduction," Josh responded proudly.

Father Anselm was very happy when the young detectives returned the stolen chalice to him. As a reward, he let them visit the library where the monks were spending the morning. Josh, David, and Lily were so tired from mystery-solving the night before, they could hardly keep their eyes open.

Lily rubbed her eyes to try to stay awake. No, it wasn't possible!

"The thief is here," she whispered to Josh and David. "See for yourselves!"

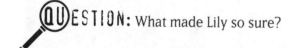 **QUESTION:** What made Lily so sure?

CLUE NINE: A Prediction

Lily counted up the monks and realized that there was one monk too many! When the phony monk realized what Lily had discovered, he dropped his books and bolted away. He ran across the library and disappeared behind a door at the back of the room. Lily ran after the man and slipped behind him just before the door closed.

The secret passage was damp and musty. Lily heard someone panting and stumbling in the darkness. She flattened herself against the wall, her heart racing. Then she let out a scream: Something was running along the side of her cheek. A spider? A cockroach? She rubbed her hands all over her face and violently shook out her hair. Suddenly a door opened at the other end of the passage, letting in a sliver of light. Lily saw the imposter disappear through the door and into the church. She was ready to take off after the thief again, but a hand on her shoulder stopped her. Father Anselm had caught up with her.

"Stop!" he said. "This isn't a game. Lily, you and your friends are great detectives, but this could be dangerous. The adults will handle things from now on. I'm going to call the police, and you should go and rejoin your friends."

Lily found Josh and David, and the three detectives waited until the monks had left to investigate the crime before they snuck back into the church.

But it was too late. The thief was gone.

"The man passed through here," Josh said as the group walked through a thin, tall doorway. "And I'm certain he's really annoyed right now."

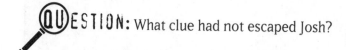 **QUESTION:** What clue had not escaped Josh?

CLUE TEN: Keep Your Eyes Peeled

The thief had accidentally dropped his glasses at the foot of the window on the right. Josh knew from experience how annoying it was to lose your glasses!

"I wonder why he risked mixing with the monks in the library," David said. "He knew we had discovered the theft and found the chalice."

"Precisely," said Father Anselm, who appeared suddenly, carrying a bucket of water in his hand. "That's why he came back. The man was desperate to get back our valuable silver chalice. Somebody probably paid him a large sum of money to steal it. These kinds of thefts happen all the time, unfortunately. What can we do besides alert the police and lock up the chalice again?" He sighed. "After lunch, children, I'd like you to water the vegetable garden. I hope that will take your mind off of all this unpleasantness."

As soon as they finished eating, Josh, David, and Lily went to the well to get water for the vegetables. After they completed the chore, they considered rolling up their pants and wading in the shallow well to cool off. Before they could, David spotted another clue.

"The thief is over there," David told his friends. "I'm sure of it. And this time, we've got him cornered!"

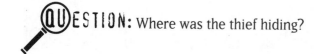 **QUESTION:** Where was the thief hiding?

CLUE ELEVEN: Another Miscount

Only the most brilliant detective would notice the detail that David had picked up: The wheel of the wheelbarrow at the back of the garden was flat! There was something big and heavy in it, weighing it down. Because of the theft, no one had worked in the garden all day, so it couldn't have been the monks who loaded it up—it had to be the thief. He was hiding in the wheelbarrow!

Alerted by Father Anselm's call, Inspector Tony Shipman arrived at the abbey with his brother, Frank. Lily brought her uncles up to speed.

"Police!" Tony announced with authority. He pointed to the wheelbarrow. "Come out with your hands up. You're trapped!"

The thief realized there was no way for him to escape. He surrendered and Tony put the cuffs on him. The three detectives ran back to the abbey to tell Father Anselm their news. The other monks told them that Father Anselm had just gone up to his room for his afternoon nap.

On their way up to Father Anselm's room, the detectives stopped to help Brother Claudius hand out tickets to a large group of tourists. They collected ticket stubs and herded the tourists into the church, where Brother Claudius planned to give the group a short history of the abbey.

But as the visitors assembled in the church, Lily had a terrible realization.

"One of the tourists is missing!" she cried.

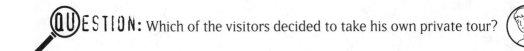 **QUESTION:** Which of the visitors decided to take his own private tour?

CLUE TWELVE: Time Is Running Out

David and Josh quickly counted the visitors to whom they had given tickets. Lily was right. The man in the hat carrying an umbrella wasn't there! They had to tell Father Anselm right away. While Brother Claudius told the visitors the history of Blackbird Rock Josh, David, and Lily climbed up the stairs and along the passageway that led to Father Anselm's cell. They knocked on the door, lightly at first, but then louder and louder. No answer. Where was he?

"I think I hear groaning, don't you?" whispered Lily. Goosebumps appeared all over her long arms.

Even though he was afraid, David pressed his eye up against the keyhole and squinted into Father Anselm's room.

"Come on, tell us what you see in there!" Josh said urgently.

"I . . . I don't know. I think Father Anselm is in danger. In any case, he or someor else is certainly in his room. Look for yourselves!"

 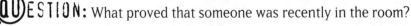**QUESTION:** What proved that someone was recently in the room?

CLUE THIRTEEN: The Phantom Patient

After taking turns looking through the keyhole, Lily and Josh saw the evidence f themselves. The hourglass on the desk had been turned upside down just a few minutes earlier—probably just before they arrived! Grains of sand trickled slowly into the botto of the hourglass. Someone must have been there recently to turn the hourglass.

The three friends ran to the kitchen, where Brother Donald was busy making dinner. Once he heard the news, he abandoned the casserole he was preparing and use his keys to unlock the door to Father Anselm's room.

"Good heavens!" he exclaimed when he saw poor Father Anselm tied to a chair i the corner of the room with a sock stuffed into his mouth. Who could have done this?

"Thank goodness you came to look for me!" Father Anselm gasped. "I went to tu over my hourglass, which I use to measure my nap time, when a masked intruder weari a monk's robe came in and attacked me. He wanted to know where we were keeping hi accomplice, but I refused to tell him. He tackled me and tied me to the chair!"

The hunt for the second intruder began. Brother Donald and Josh, David, and Li were on the case. The kids wanted to investigate the abbey's old infirmary.

"Don't waste your time there," Brother Donald told them. "The infirmary has bee abandoned for years."

Lily didn't believe him. She peeked into the room through a dusty window.

"A waste of time? I don't think so," Lily said triumphantly. "Someone was just here!"

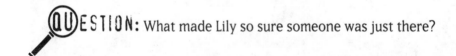

QUESTION: What made Lily so sure someone was just there?

CLUE FOURTEEN: A Bloody Blow

In the back of the room, there was a half-filled glass of water on a small table. Josh deduced that this was where the thief hid before stealing the chalice. But where wa his partner?

David reached for the infirmary's doorknob when—*BAM!*—the door swung open and hit him right in the face. As David cried out in pain, a man in a robe bolted from the infirmary and took off at top speed toward the emergency exit.

Brother Donald caught up to him, but the intruder spun around, tripped the poo monk, and took off. Josh gave his handkerchief to David to clean up his bloody nose, an Lily helped Brother Donald to his feet.

"Burry up! Be've got to catch him!" shouted David, his nose muffled by the blood soaked handkerchief.

"Don't chase him!" ordered Brother Donald. "This man seems to know the area very well. It's useless to run after him. It might be better to set a trap."

"Great idea," said Lily. She showed Brother Donald a slip of paper she had picke up off the ground. "But the man trapped himself by dropping this piece of paper. He's planning to go to the circus tomorrow afternoon. What do you say, gang?"

"Let's go!" exclaimed Josh. "I'm sure I'll recognize him, even though I didn't see his face. There's one particular detail that will give him away."

The next day, the three friends went to the circus's matinee performance. Durin the elephant parade, Josh elbowed his friends. He had found the thief's accomplice!

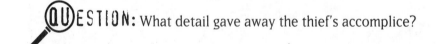

QUESTION: What detail gave away the thief's accomplice?

Calinero Circus
tomorro
3:00

CLUE FIFTEEN: A Tidy Solution

The man was seated in the third row, in the shadows. His face was buried in his program. Josh recognized him because while most men wear their wristwatches on their left hands, he wore his on his right. Josh had noticed this detail yesterday as they were chasing him.

"He probably had a meeting with someone, but who?" Lily wondered. "It can't be the thief, because Tony already arrested him."

"Maybe it's the person who paid the thief to steal the chalice," suggested David.

The three friends hid near the exit of the circus tent. When the accomplice left the circus, the detectives would get him. But the accomplice knew what the detectives were up to. He hid among the crowd as hundreds of people poured out of the big top. The kids searched the crowd, but there was no sign of him. They were about to give up hope, when David's face lit up.

"There he is!" he exclaimed. "It's incredible, he's already changed disguises. We can't let him get away again!"

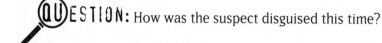

QUESTION: How was the suspect disguised this time?

CLUE SIXTEEN: Breathless

After recognizing the three detectives, the phony street cleaner stuck his broom under his arm, grabbed his rolling garbage can, and started running away.

They followed the street cleaner to Fairgrounds Lane, where they saw him turn left at Alley Way.

"Hurry!" shouted David. "He's getting away!"

"Don't worry," said Josh, "Alley Way is a dead-end street."

The street was indeed a dead end, but when they reached the entrance, there was nothing there except the garbage can and Robinson the cockatoo, flying around. There was no trace of the street cleaner.

Suddenly, they heard a loud sound. Robinson screeched. Lily, David, and Josh jumped up, prepared to seize the villain. False alarm! It was just a cat that overturned a few empty bottles when he tried to get his paws on Robinson. The detectives exhaled, but Robinson was more agitated than ever. He let out another big screech and furiously flapped his wings. David looked carefully at the scene and then turned to his friends.

"Robinson figured out where the fugitive is hiding. This time, we've got him!"

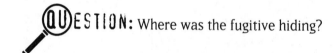 **QUESTION:** Where was the fugitive hiding?

CLUE SEVENTEEN: The Fallen Angel

David signaled to Lily and Josh to follow him. They crouched in front of the thief's hiding place and waited, counting the seconds. The man couldn't hold on much longer. Exactly twenty-nine seconds later, the street cleaner's head emerged from the water barrel. His face was purple and dripping. Gasping for breath, he spat out a huge stream of water he had swallowed while underwater. Before the thief had time to make another escape, David backed him into a corner with his street cleaner's broom.

When Frank and Tony arrived on the scene moments later, they found themselves face-to-face with a soggy, pale man whose teeth were chattering.

"Please," he begged them, "get this dirty broom off of me!"

The suspect accepted a handkerchief from Tony, wiped his face, and then tried to convince the detectives he was innocent. When Tony asked him about the garbage can, which was loaded with precious artifacts, he shrugged his shoulders. "I'm a street cleaner. I sweep up whatever I see, whether it's valuable or not. I don't decide what people throw away."

Lily decided to call his bluff. She fished a baroque statue of an angel out of the trash can.

"You're a very thorough street cleaner. You swept all the way to the abbey of Blackbird Rock!"

All the blood drained from the culprit's face.

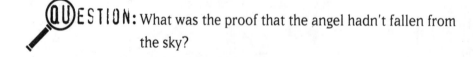

QUESTION: What was the proof that the angel hadn't fallen from the sky?

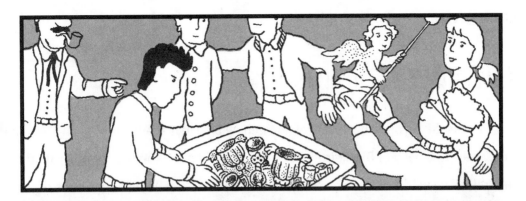

CLUE ONE: The Rabbit's Tale

It was the second angel, part of a matching pair that should have been alongside the organ at the Abbey of Blackbird Rock. The thief and his accomplice, who made their living trafficking works of art, were brought to justice. Father Anselm gave each of the young detectives a small hourglass as a way of saying thank you and Brother Donald made them a raspberry tart. The kids promised to keep in touch and visit again next year.

Case closed—for now! The friends hoped a new mystery would pop up soon for them to solve. Just their luck: It started that very afternoon at the town's annual purebred rabbit exhibition and show. The winning rabbit was awarded the Lapina Prize: ten times its weight in carrots and a yearlong subscription to *Raise My Rabbit* magazine.

After the show, Lily, David, and Josh watched the crowd pass by the rabbits' cages from a nearby balcony. Josh took his binoculars out to admire the rabbits. Suddenly he cried, "Hurry! Someone just broke into one of the cages!"

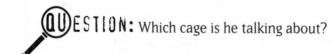 **QUESTION:** Which cage is he talking about?

CLUE TWO: A Bitter Victory

The three friends pushed their way through the crowd and stopped in front of cage number 873. Lily investigated the padlock.

"Josh is right," she said. "Someone stole this rabbit! Look, the lock was cut!"

"And this is the rabbit that just won the Lapina Prize!" David added.

"How do you know?" asked Josh.

"All you have to do is read," David explained. "I can even tell you what the rabbit's name is."

"Maurice the Magnificent!" Lily exclaimed as she read the ID tag attached to the rabbit's cage. "Hurry up, we need to tell security! With any luck, we'll be able to stop the thief before he leaves the show."

A few minutes later, the exits were locked, and all the remaining people at the show were politely asked to open their bags for inspection. But not a trace, not a single rabbit foot, was found.

"I guess now we have to find the owner and tell him the bad news," said David. "We should call him over the loudspeaker."

"That won't be necessary," Lily said with a big smile. "I can see him from here. All you have to do is look."

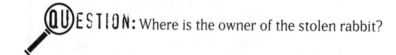 QUESTION: Where is the owner of the stolen rabbit?

CLUE THREE: A Discovery

On the sign announcing Mr. Trenton's rabbit, Maurice the Magnificent, just outside the arches of the hall on the left, you could see Mr. Trenton's picture. Josh recognized him by his round glasses and big mustache. He was sitting at a big table in the back of the room with the competition's judges. When he learned about the theft of his beloved Maurice, Mr. Trenton clutched at his heart. His bushy mustache started to quiver.

"If I catch that thief," he vowed, "I will make him eat an entire box of carrots, leaves first!"

"My friends and I will do everything we can to bring Maurice back alive," Lily pledged, tears brimming in her eyes.

Mr. Trenton's face softened, and he sighed. "That's very nice of you, kids. I don't think Maurice's life is in danger. The thief probably just wants to resell him. Maurice is worth a lot of money, you know."

David showed Josh a little piece of paper that he had picked up from the bottom of Maurice's cage.

"I think this is a piece of the label of a fancy bottle of olive oil," Josh explained. "Look, here's half of the label. It has some weird symbol on it. It must be the brand's logo."

Josh found a copy of the Yellow Pages and wrote down the addresses of all the gourmet shops in town that sold specialty olive oils. The next day, they visited all the shops that they found. As the detectives studied the window of the third gourmet grocery store they had on their list, Josh cried, "Good work, David! We found the right bottle!"

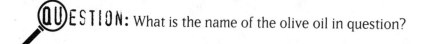 **QUESTION:** What is the name of the olive oil in question?

CLUE FOUR: Down the Rabbit Hole

Josh stood on his tiptoes to see what David had found on the very last shelf of the gourmet shop.

"Fiery Pepper Oil, twenty dollars," he read from the bottle. The logo on its label exactly matched the label half they had found in Maurice's cage.

"You don't actually think that this gourmet shop has something to do with the theft, do you?" Lily asked. She was beginning to think this whole idea was a little ridiculous, and she wanted some time to think. "Let's go have a meeting at the Sugar Shack."

The boys reluctantly followed her out of the store. But before they reached the Sugar Shack, the boys stopped in front of a poster advertising a horror movie. As Lily told Josh and David to hurry up, she noticed something strange. She took out Josh's binoculars from her backpack. No, she wasn't dreaming. Lily called Josh and David over.

"Oh, wow!" said Josh, looking through the binoculars.

"That's incredible!" added David, taking his turn.

"You were right," Lily admitted.

Thanks to pure luck, the investigation was back on track.

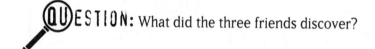

QUESTION: What did the three friends discover?

CLUE FIVE: Crunched!

Among the packages stored on the back of the mail truck, Lily saw a big box labeled "Fiery Pepper Oil." And that wasn't all! Looking very closely through Josh's binoculars, she noticed that someone had punched lots of little holes in the top of the box—air holes to allow an animal to breathe! There wasn't a moment to lose! The friends tried to run across the street to the mail truck, but the light suddenly changed to green and a path of speeding cars blocked their way and stopped them.

Trapped on the other side of the street, they watched helplessly as the mailman picked up the box and carried it away. He disappeared behind the door of a building. The light turned red and the friends ran across the street. They walked up to the door of the building where the mailman had disappeared.

"Now what?" Josh whispered. "We can't ring every doorbell, can we? David, what are you doing?"

David had discovered a tall ladder in the corner of the building's courtyard and signaled to the others to help him place it against the wall of the building. They climbed the ladder and peered into the window to their right on the second floor. They saw a dentist hard at work, but there was no evidence of Maurice. Next, they looked into the window on the left.

"Get down from there, you rascals!" the landlady of the building screamed.

The three detectives scrambled down the ladder and raced down the street. They had seen enough: They found Maurice's trail!

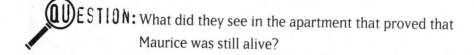

QUESTION: What did they see in the apartment that proved that Maurice was still alive?

CLUE SIX: A Man Goes Shopping

"Phew! That was close," Josh said once he was sure that the landlady wasn't following them.

"Let's keep going," said Lily. "Maurice is being held prisoner in the apartment we saw through the window. I'm sure we all noticed the half-eaten carrot on the kitchen floor. Now we know that the thief lives in this buil—"

She stopped speaking abruptly. She saw that the door of the building had opened. Out walked a man wearing a hat. In his left hand, he held a picnic basket, and in his right hand, he was balancing the box they had seen on the mail truck! He walked to the dumpster on the corner and threw away the box. Then he walked toward the center of town.

David, Josh, and Lily followed a little bit behind him, very careful not to let him see them. After a while, the man entered a sporting goods store. Through the store window, the friends watched as the man selected a backpack, paid for it, and put it in the bottom of his picnic basket. He left the store and continued on his way.

But the street was so crowded that the detectives lost sight of him. They decided to split up so they would have a better chance of finding him, and planned to meet up again in five minutes at the flower shop on the corner.

"I know where he is," Josh said, once the detectives met up again after searching for the man separately. "Come quickly!"

 **QUESTION:** Where did Josh find the man with the hat?

CLUE SEVEN: It Moves!

"Here are your carrots, sir," the grocer said to the man with the basket. "Anythin
else?"

"That's all," said the man. He paid for his food, and walked away from the fruit
and vegetable stand. The three detectives decided it was too risky to follow him back
to his apartment, so they took a different route back to his building. They arrived there
before he did, so they waited in front of the Sugar Shack across the street, pretending to
be interested in the candy in the window.

"Look, there he is!" Lily whispered as she spied his reflection in the window. "He'
going into the building."

"Great," said Josh. "Now what do we do?"

It was a good question. No one answered. The friends were out of ideas.

"Wait, he's coming back out with his backpack!" cried David.

Josh, David, and Lily crossed the street and followed the man onto a bus. His
backpack appeared to be wiggling! After thirty minutes, the man got off at the second-to-
last stop, next to a farm that was near a forest.

Lily and Josh got up to follow him, but David stopped them—the farm was so
isolated, it would be obvious that they were following him. They stayed on the bus until
the last stop, and then got back on the bus going the other direction toward town. When
they got off at the stop by the farm, they saw a fence surrounding the entire property.

"I see evidence of hungry bunnies!" said Lily, peering over the fence.

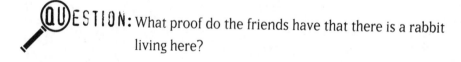 **QUESTION:** What proof do the friends have that there is a rabbit
living here?

CLUE EIGHT: The Rabbit with Little Polka Dots

Two beautiful pumpkins grew at the back of the yard, and one of them had been nibbled!

"Okay," Josh said. "So there could be rabbits at this farm, and they could have eaten the pumpkin. That's nothing extraordinary, right? How do we know the man brought Maurice here? Plus, I don't see any rabbits."

Lily and David suddenly dashed off. "Hey! Wait for me!" Josh ran after them. He caught up with his friends just as they approached a hole in the fence. David looked through it. He began to chuckle when he saw the crowd of happy rabbits on the other side.

"Come look, Josh. I don't think you'll be disappointed."

Josh crouched down and looked through the hole in the fence. "Wow! I've never seen so many bunnies in one place! They're so cute! And all different! Do you have the picture of Maurice, David?"

David handed Josh a newspaper article with Maurice's picture. The three friends looked very closely at the photo. Then they looked at the rabbits one by one, until they came to an agreement. Maurice was certainly there!

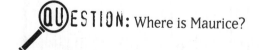 QUESTION: Where is Maurice?

CLUE NINE: After Much Consideration . . .

The rabbit in the photo had three black spots on each side, black ears, and a black tail. And he was sitting at the far end of the yard, sniffing a drainpipe.

"Let's see if he responds to his name," said Josh, calling him quietly. Maurice turned toward Josh.

"Hooray!" yelled Lily, patting Josh on the back.

"Don't celebrate yet! How are we going to get him out of here?" Josh asked.

"Easy! We'll sneak in and grab him," said Lily. She started to climb the fence, and the two boys followed.

The confused rabbits watched as the detectives dropped onto the soft grass on the other side of the fence. The kids looked around to make sure no one saw them, then carefully moved toward the kidnapped rabbit. Lily reached out to grab Maurice, but he became afraid and slipped out of her grip. In three hops, Maurice disappeared into the barn.

"It's going to be difficult to find him in there," David whispered.

"Shhhh!" Josh interrupted him. "I hear footsteps."

The detectives quickly hid behind some giant sacks of potatoes. The footsteps came closer and closer to the barn. Josh turned to Lily and whispered, "I know where Maurice is hiding! Look closely and you'll see!"

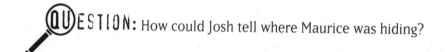 **QUESTION:** How could Josh tell where Maurice was hiding?

CLUE TEN: Robinson and the Rabbit

Lily looked everywhere, but she could not find Maurice. Josh pointed him out: He was hidden in one side of the old and broken scale on the table in the back corner of the barn. Josh saw the tops of Maurice's ears, and noticed that his weight had made the scale tip.

"Achoo!!!"

The friends jumped. Someone had sneezed very loudly from just outside the barn door. The three friends peered out the doorway. The man with the hat putting his handkerchief back in his pocket was . . .

"Larkin!" David exclaimed, remembering the name written on the sign outside the farm.

Robinson cawed loudly. "Shh! Robinson! Be quiet!" hushed Josh. The cockatoo ignored him and chased Maurice, who had left his hiding place and hopped off to join his bunny friends.

"What now?" Lily wondered.

David replied, "If Larkin is hiding Maurice here, he must be waiting for money."

"You mean he's looking for someone to sell him to?" asked Josh.

"Or he's already found someone," Lily declared. "I think Larkin may be negotiating with someone right now."

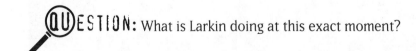

QUESTION: What is Larkin doing at this exact moment?

CLUE ELEVEN: In the Shadow of Bear Rock

David and Josh looked where Lily was pointing. Larkin was on the telephone.

"Oh, look, he hung up," Josh said. "And he looks really happy. He must have gotten good news. He's putting on his hat . . . Look out! Hide!"

The detectives dove behind a pile of wood as Larkin headed toward their hiding place. Luckily, he passed within inches of the detectives without noticing them. Larkin carried a basket of cabbage leaves and whistled as he walked toward the rabbit pen.

"Let's get out of here," David said, and they ran past Larkin and up to the house. They peered through the window. On the table by the telephone, they saw a handwritten note. It read: "Five o'clock. The zoo."

Josh looked at his watch. "It's 4:43 now, so the meeting must be tomorrow."

The next day, minutes before five o'clock, the detectives waited outside of the Hillsdale Zoo with Frank and Tony.

"Your trip to the farm wasn't exactly legal," Tony grumbled. "Don't do that again, okay?"

The detectives nodded as they entered the zoo. They paused at the top of the pathway that led to the sea animals' tank. Frank turned to David, Josh, and Lily and asked, "Do you have any idea where Larkin is meeting his friend?"

"Um . . . not really," David admitted.

"Look!" Lily cried. She was spying through her binoculars at Larkin walking through the zoo. "I see Larkin! And look at the man next to him! Don't you recognize him?"

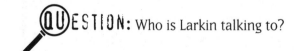 **QUESTION:** Who is Larkin talking to?

Five
O' Clock
The Zoo

WELCOME

CLUE TWELVE: The Carrots Are Cooked!

The detectives could not believe their eyes: The man with the big mustache standing with Larkin between the bears and the lions was none other than Mr. Trenton!

"That's unbelievable!" cried Josh. "What a liar! Do you remember how upset he pretended to be when we told him that someone had stolen Maurice? Come on, let's hid and confront him when the moment is right."

The detectives, Frank, and Tony tiptoed closer to the two men and hid behind the bear's rocks. They could hear Larkin and Mr. Trenton's conversation perfectly. The two had been plotting together the whole time: The theft was staged by Mr. Trenton, wh wanted the insurance money!

"You've done a very good job," the group overheard Trenton say to Larkin. "I'm pleased with your work. And don't forget! When Maurice becomes a father again, I wan the three prettiest baby bunnies."

"I won't forget," said Larkin, taking the suitcase Trenton handed him. "Good-bye

This was their chance! The detectives sprang from their hiding place. Larkin sensed the danger and ran away, but Trenton froze with fear. Tony apprehended Trenton and led him out of the zoo. He locked him in his squad car and went back to join the others as they chased Larkin. The group found Larkin high in a tree overlooking the elephant building. Larkin had already hidden the suitcase filled with money somewhere else.

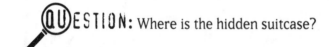 **QUESTION:** Where is the hidden suitcase?

CLUE ONE: Introducing Arabella

Larkin left the suitcase filled with money in the elephant building before climbin up the tree. And it was filled with rolls of quarters!

"Not very practical to carry, but harder to trace than bills, which have serial numbers," the police officer at the station explained to them after the friends turned the thief over to him.

"To thank you for closing this case, here are three tickets to tomorrow night's concert in the city. Sadly, I can't go because I have to work, but I want you to enjoy them."

The friends thanked him and opened the envelope.

"Recital of the Operatic Works of Arabella Ducoffre, soprano," David read. The policeman proudly explained, "Arabella and I went to school together, and she's a famous opera singer now. She has an international career, but she's never forgotten me

"Opera?" Lily said when they left the police station. "I don't think I like opera."

"We have to go—it's a gift! Plus, we'll get to go to the city," Josh pointed out.

The next night, the three friends dressed in their nicest clothes and met up at the theater. The curtain went up, the pianist played the opening notes of "Nightingale, Sick with Love," and Arabella began to sing in a beautiful voice. However, during the firs few lines of the song, her voice cut in and out over the loudspeaker. The engineer in charge of the show jumped out of his seat and ran backstage. Right away, Lily knew why "Someone is trying to sabotage the show!" she whispered to Josh.

 **QUESTION:** What did Lily see?

CLUE TWO: Ducoffre Disappeared

The microphone cord had been cut! But Arabella wouldn't let that stop her. She told the audience, "My voice doesn't need a microphone! The show must go on! I owe it to my public." The audience applauded loudly, and Arabella continued to sing.

Arabella sang every note perfectly. Everyone seemed to have forgotten about th incident with the cut microphone cord. Everyone, that is, except the three detectives.

The next afternoon, they decided to visit Arabella at her townhouse. They deciced to tell her they wanted to interview her for their school newspaper. Josh, David and Lily parked their bikes outside her home and rang the doorbell. The groundskeeper, Mr. Dobbs, let them in. He looked worried.

"My poor children," he said, frazzled. "Ms. Ducoffre has disappeared! But please come in while I tell you the story!" He led them to the veranda that looked out over the garden.

"At 12:30 this afternoon, I arrived to deliver the newspaper—the reviews of Ms. Ducoffre's performance were wonderful! When I arrived, I found the door to the verand wide open. That seemed unusual to me, because Ms. Ducoffre doesn't like a breeze in he home; she says it gives her a sore throat. I was also worried because Doremi, her parrot, was completely silent. He never leaves her side when she's home. Oh my! What is that bird doing?"

The question was directed at David, who had Robinson perched on his shoulder.

"He's investigating," David smiled. "And I think he's found Doremi."

 **QUESTION:** Where was Arabella Ducoffre's parrot hiding?

CLUE THREE: The Parrot's Accent

Robinson flew to the watering can next to the bench. He exchanged a few friendly parrot words with Doremi, who finally came out of his hiding place. Mr. Dobbs poured two big bowls of peanuts and dried fruit, and called to the birds. They flew to Doremi's perch and pecked away at the food happily.

"My brave little Doremi, I'm so happy I found you again," said Mr. Dobbs, petting the bird's head with his index finger. "And your mistress? Can you tell us where she is?"

"Does he talk?" asked Lily.

In response, Doremi shook his head, opened his beak wide, and started squawking in a shrill voice, "ITWU ZDA CAW FEEDAT HERTDHUR!"

"Articulate, Doremi!" cried Mr. Dobbs. "No one understands what you're saying!"

Annoyed, the parrot closed his beak.

"Keep going, Doremi," said David gently, taking out his notebook and a pen. The parrot repeated the strange noises, and David wrote down everything he heard.

After a little thinking, Josh suddenly cried, "I've got it!"

 **QUESTION:** What message was Doremi trying to communicate?

CLUE FOUR: Asleep on Her Feet

"It was the coffee that hurt her," David repeated. "But what coffee are you talkin about, Doremi?"

"Probably this," said Lily, pointing to a half-full cup on the breakfast table. She picked it up and sniffed it. Doremi started squawking again.

"I think we're on the right path," Lily said as she put the coffee down. She picked up a small vial Josh had found near the door to the veranda and sniffed it. "It's the same smell!" she exclaimed. "Whatever went in the coffee came from this vial. Let's take this t the pharmacy for analysis."

Gavin Connolly, the pharmacist, was on the phone when they arrived. He held u one finger to ask them to wait while he finished his phone call. His conversation took a long time. David pulled impatiently on Lily's sleeve. "Let's go."

"Why? It will just take a minute," she replied.

"We don't need to have the vial analyzed after all. Someone definitely put something in Arabella's coffee. And I know exactly what it was."

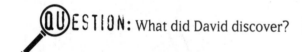 **QUESTION:** What did David discover?

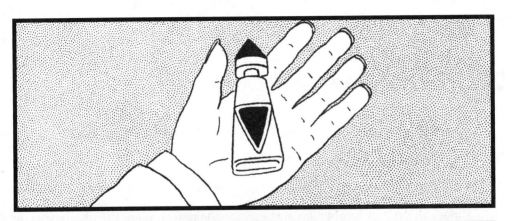

CLUE FIVE: The Latest News

Josh and Lily followed David's gaze. There, on the top shelf, under a sign marked "SEDATIVES," was a bottle exactly like the one Lily held in her hand.

"A sedative?" Josh asked. "What is that, exactly?"

"A medication that treats pain and cures insomnia," replied the pharmacist, who had just hung up the phone. "It makes you sleepy." The three friends thanked him and left the pharmacy. They knew enough.

"Someone must have put a heavy dose of that sedative in Arabella Ducoffre's coffee to put her to sleep," David guessed.

"So they could kidnap her," added Josh. "But why?"

"That's what we have to figure out," said Lily. "Maybe to ask for ransom money?" She looked over at Josh, who had an odd expression on his face. "What's wrong?"

"She's coming back," he replied.

"Who is?" Lily asked.

"The missing opera singer! Look! It's written right over there!"

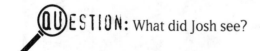 **QUESTION:** What did Josh see?

CLUE SIX: A Strange Return

There it was, printed at the top of the newspaper: Arabella Ducoffre was moving to Hillsdale! She was arriving by train the following day.

The detectives were perplexed. Why would Arabella give up her international career for life in the small town of Hillsdale? Why did she suddenly disappear from her townhouse in the city? Was she really drugged, or was it just a setup? And for what?

The next day the three friends went to the train station to wait for the singer. A crowd of reporters hoping for interviews was there, too. Once her train arrived, Arabella greeted her adoring fans and stopped to answer the journalists' questions. Ronald Crenning, a young reporter, followed her through the station.

"One final question, ma'am," Ronald said. "In which hotel are you staying?"

"I wouldn't count on me to tell you, young man," she said, smiling sweetly.

"How are we going to find her, then?" Josh whispered to Lily.

"Easy as pie," smiled Lily. "I happen to know where she's going."

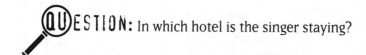

QUESTION: In which hotel is the singer staying?

CLUE SEVEN: Before and After

When Arabella left the train, Lily had noticed that her suitcase had a checkered pattern. The chauffeur for the Hotel Odeon had put this suitcase in the trunk of his car.

The detectives ran to catch the bus, which took them to the middle of town, only a few minutes from the Hotel Odeon.

"Look! There she is!" David shouted, pointing to Arabella. She exited the hotel after changing her outfit and dropping off her bags.

They detectives followed Arabella through the streets of the old part of town. Eventually, Arabella came to an antique shop famous for its valuable pieces.

"What is she doing in there?" Josh asked, after waiting outside the store for a half-hour. "Nothing in there is worth this much time!"

While the detectives waited, the shop owner redecorated the display in her store window. After she removed pieces of jewelry and furniture from her old display, she carefully dusted and polished them, and then rearranged them in the store window. All this work meant she wasn't able to spend time in the store with Arabella as she browsed.

Finally, Arabella left the store. But she was empty-handed. She bid a quick good-bye to the shop owner and hurried down the street.

As the owner closed the door, she gazed proudly at her newly decorated window then suddenly looked alarmed.

"Oh, no!" said David, who could picture exactly how the window used to look. "Something's missing, and Arabella took it!"

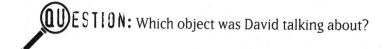 **QUESTION:** Which object was David talking about?

Mary Asher's Antiques
since 1972

CLUE EIGHT: First to the Left, Then to the Right

"Yes, of course!" cried Lily. "You're right, David. The crystal bottle that was on th
top shelf is missing."

"Maybe our singer is a kleptomaniac," suggested David. "She's someone who can
stop herself from stealing."

"Great," said Josh, grimacing. "But where does that leave our case?"

The three detectives then decided to go back to Arabella's townhouse to look
for more clues. But when they got there, they saw that the curtains were closed and the
house was dark. A neighbor informed them that Dobbs, the groundskeeper, had gone to
visit his sick mother. "And he brought the parrot with him," she added. "What a
nice man!"

Two days later, the local news published an article about Arabella, accompanied
by a picture of her. Lily picked up the paper and read: "The behavior of opera singer
Arabella Ducoffre has been odd lately. Yesterday Ms. Ducoffre claimed that the hot
chocolate she ordered at Art Café was cold, so she angrily knocked over her table. Later
that evening, at the Harvest Dinner, she tripped the waiter who served her apple cider
and accused him of trying to poison her."

Finally, there was something new to investigate! They caught up with Arabella
outside the Hillsdale Theater. A boy asked the star for an autograph for his father. She
gladly gave it to him.

But as Josh watched what was happening, he told his friends, "That person is not
Arabella Ducoffre, and we have proof!"

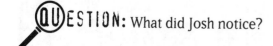 **QUESTION:** What did Josh notice?

CLUE NINE: Find the Intruder!

Arabella Ducoffre was left-handed, as the picture in the newspaper clearly showed. However, this woman was signing an autograph with her right hand!

"So she's an imposter!" whispered Lily. "And we let her fool us!"

"This is strong evidence," said David. "Now that we know this woman who we've been following isn't actually Arabella Ducoffre, we know for sure that the real Arabella has disappeared."

"Don't you think it's time for the police to get involved? Let's go get Tony!" Josh urged.

"No, let's wait until tomorrow," David proposed. He didn't want to give up the case just yet.

David was right, because the next day the newspaper published Ronald Crenning's story. It was filled with pictures of the phony Arabella and a story that the singer had lost her voice.

"That's a rumor and a lie!" Lily exclaimed. "Those pictures aren't even of the real Arabella! Do you guys notice anything funny about these pictures?"

Intrigued, Josh and David peered over her shoulder. Suddenly, Josh cried, "Oh, wow! I hadn't noticed before! That can't be just a coincidence!"

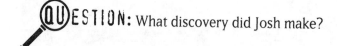 **QUESTION:** What discovery did Josh make?

CLUE TEN: The Woman in the Shadows

Who was the woman in black who appeared alongside Arabella in all seven photos? The detectives called Ronald Crenning to ask. His answer made them even more curious: "That woman is Helen Apens, Arabella's former assistant and hairdresser. Arabella fired her some time ago. Since then, she's been working for another singer, Jessica Ceyrol, a real screecher from what I've heard."

Ronald Crenning thought it was odd that Arabella's fired assistant was in the photos, and so did the young detectives. They had to find Helen Apens. First, they went to the Hotel Odeon and asked if Helen was a guest there. "Sorry," the receptionist told them. "Our hotel doesn't give out information about our guests."

"Helen Apens is staying here all right," Lily whispered. "I even know which room she's in. Come on, let's take the elevator. With any luck, we can probably get a peek at her room while she's out."

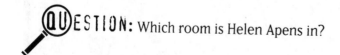 **QUESTION:** Which room is Helen Apens in?

CLUE ELEVEN: Nlocnil Yerffej

David had noticed a letter addressed to H. Apens, room 217, in the mailbox behind the receptionist's counter. The detectives took the elevator to the second floor, and when they got there saw that the maid was just leaving Room 217 to get more towels and the door was still wide open. Except for the maid, the room—and the hallway—were completely empty.

"Sneak in and take a look around, guys," said Josh. "I'll stay here and keep watch."

David and Lily quietly snuck into the room, but they weren't even sure what to look for. Plus, they felt uncomfortable about sneaking into her room. After a few moments, David and Lily noticed a very strange business card peeking out of a book on the nightstand.

"NLOCNIL YERFFEJ," Lily read. "TEERTS EKAC 8, ELLIVNEERG." She took out her notebook and wrote down what was written on the card. Then David and Lily heard Josh clear his throat loudly in the hallway—the signal that someone was coming. They ran out of the room and, once they were safely in the hallway, showed Josh the note in Lily's notebook. Josh didn't understand what it meant.

David said, "It's a simple question of common sense."

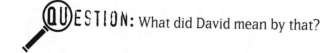 **QUESTION:** What did David mean by that?

CLUE TWELVE: A Troubling Discovery

Josh did what David suggested and looked at the letters again. Soon, the mysterious words made sense.

"Jeffrey Lincoln, 8 Cake Street, Greenville," he read aloud. "But why did Jeffrey Lincoln take the time to spell the words on his business card backward?"

"That's what we need to find out," said Lily. "Helen Apens and Jeffrey Lincoln are clearly working together, but what are they up to?"

The little village of Greenville, famous for its delicious cakes, was twenty miles north of Hillsdale. At the train station, the three detectives hopped on a bus. Forty-five minutes later, they were in front of the mayor's office. Cake Street was very close by. Number 8 Cake Street, they discovered, was named Chestnut Cottage, a pretty house with a garden. They stood by the gate and observed the property. The house seemed to be deserted. Cautiously, the three friends walked through the overgrown garden and up to the front door.

"Is anyone home?" Lily called out.

Everything was silent. David shrugged. "Another dead end. Come on, let's go home."

"Not so fast," said Josh. "Something is wrong here. Look, there's proof!"

 **QUESTION:** What did Josh discover?

CLUE THIRTEEN: Between Old Barrels and Bottles

The three friends approached the wheelbarrow where Josh had noticed a gun lying on a bed of straw.

"Don't touch it!" cried David. "It could be loaded."

"Of course we won't touch it!" Lily answered. "We know how dangerous guns are."

"Yes, David's right," said Josh. "Guns are really dangerous. Plus, if we touch it, we could smudge the fingerprints on it, and then we wouldn't be able to identify the owner of the gun . . ."

"Who is probably Jeffrey Lincoln," Lily finished. "Here's what we have so far: Arabella Ducoffre disappears mysteriously, and a look-alike takes her place and ruins her reputation. Then there's Helen Apens, who Arabella fired as her assistant. Helen probably wanted revenge, so she made Arabella disappear and found the look-alike to impersonate Arabella. And Jeffrey Lincoln probably helped Helen. But what have they done to Arabella? Maybe there's a clue here."

Josh inspected the well at the back of the garden. Lily looked behind the pile of firewood. David wiped off the grimy basement window. Suddenly, he signaled to the others.

"Are you guys seeing what I'm seeing?" he murmured uneasily.

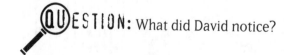 **QUESTION:** What did David notice?

CLUE FOURTEEN: Garbage and a Car Chase

Josh and Lily looked around. What they saw in the basement made them shudder. Behind the barrel on the right-hand side of the shelf, they saw a woman's feet and the bottom of her dress.

"D-do you guys th-th-think that sh-she's . . . d-dead?" Josh stammered.

David whipped his cell phone out and dialed Tony's number while Lily kicked through the basement window. A few minutes later, the detectives crawled through the window and into the basement. In front of them, bound, gagged, and bruised—but alive-was the real Arabella Ducoffre. The detectives took off her gag, untied her, and helped her to her feet. The singer told them that a masked man had taken her hostage.

"Can you remember anything that happened the day you were taken?" Lily asked.

"All I can remember is that my old assistant came to see me while I was eating breakfast one morning. She came to ask my forgiveness. I fired her because . . ."

Arabella's explanation was interrupted by the sound of car doors slamming. The three friends ran outside to greet Tony and Frank. Another car pulled up behind them a few minutes later, but quickly drove away after noticing Tony's squad car. The group piled into Tony's car and chased after the other car—they had a feeling the kidnapper was behind the wheel.

They followed the other car to a garbage dump. The road suddenly ended, and Jeffrey Lincoln jumped out of the car and dove into the piles of garbage and disappeared.

"Police! Come out, you're surrounded!" cried Tony.

"Don't worry, we've got him. I can see him," said Frank, pointing.

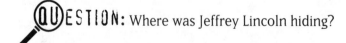 **QUESTION:** Where was Jeffrey Lincoln hiding?

CLUE FIFTEEN: The Truth Comes Out

Jeffrey Lincoln was in the middle of the garbage pile, hidden between a library bookshelf, a chair, and a bicycle. Jeffrey didn't put up any resistance when Tony handcuffed him and brought him to the police station—he knew he was trapped. He even gave a full confession of his guilt, which also incriminated Helen Apens. Jeffrey told the detectives, "She looked sad. She told me that her boss ruined her life by firing her unfairly, and that she had to be punished for that. And I, poor fool, am so in love with Helen that I believed her! Oh, women are so cruel!"

When questioned, Arabella told a completely different story. "I caught Helen stealing my annotated musical scores, my most prized possessions. She was going to sell them to some second-rate singer. That's why I fired her." Arabella looked exhausted and close to tears. Tony drove her home and told her to rest.

"Please," he said to the singer. "Don't go out in public for a little while. Helen Apens cannot find out that you've been freed."

Later that day, the three detectives met at the Sugar Shack. They studied the performance schedule for the theater downtown. They couldn't believe it: The fake Arabella was performing!

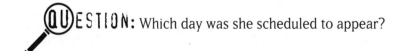 **QUESTION:** Which day was she scheduled to appear?

MUNICIPAL THEATER SCHEDULE FOR JULY

July 1st The Masked Devil:
by Maurice Quetou with Eva Nouvel, Adam Wolf, and Lucy Ferris

July 2nd The Enchanted Forest:
by Merlin Pimpin with Chantal Isment and Claire Delune and Lulu

July 3rd The Thief's Lover:
by Dawn Alamour with Amandine Happy Independence Fever: Fireworks, games, and performances

July 4th Independence Fever:
Fireworks, games, and performances

July 5th Max and Folly:
The famous clown duo performs acrobatics and juggling

July 6th The White Unicorn:
Operetta by Angela Limier, with Patsy Bryce, Rose Swan, Gordon Blue, and Laura Pettit

July 7th The Inspector Sees Double:
Comedy-Thriller by Constantine Mirot with Stindall Twins

July 8th The Brothers Caramelov:
Tragedy by Theodore Pele with Eva Nussbaum, Ella Froy, and Yvon Jones

July 9th The Barrel of Monkeys:
Comic Opera by Albin Defoule, with Melissa Mollyglot, Patrick Louche, and Rene Johnson

July 10th The Castaways of Mars:
by Lucas Lamitay, with Francesca Lane, Sally Westinghouse, and Sebastian Clancy

July 11th The Happy Sled:
by Emily Fields with Elsa Dragoudis, Elvira Smart, and Maeve Bowers

July 12th Ace of Spades:
by Icarus Judice with Susan Hart, Narcissa James, and Joe Conan

July 13th The Kid's Place:
A celebration of summer vacation. Free admission. Bring all your friends.

July 14th Fire from the Dragon:
by Peter Briquet with Monica Lume, Philippa Foot, and Adele Letain

July 15th Harlequin Has a Party:
Marionnette show by the Company of the Crazy Kings

July 16th The Wizard Who Loved Me:
Melodrama in three acts by Armand Nyme with Alba Broussard, Yvette Anwat

July 17th A Midsummer Night's Dream: by William Shakespeare by the Royal Shakespeare Society of Stratford-upon-Avon

July 18th Eternal Egypt:
Conference and discussion led by Profesor Miriam Cessedeux from the Institute of Antiquities

July 19th Who's that Crane?:
The extraordinary adventures of Mimi the Crane, music by Felicity Coyne

July 20th Fairies and Magic Spells:
Magic show presented by the Houdini Association with Blanche Applebaum and Claire Komelo

July 21st Shadow Man:
by Eddy Sparrow with Aisha Dos, Emma Gladstone, and Geoffrey Spader

July 22nd The Venetian Mask:
Comic opera by Alonzo T. Atre with Isabelle Cache

July 23rd The Miller's Daughters:
A musical comedy by Claire Fontaine with Laura Prileau Lola Temple and Va

July 24th Kidnapped:
Opera in one act by Ameli Lascar with Arabella Ducoffre, Pascale Feely, Vincent Fandino, and Mark James. Conducted Ingrid Rodriguez

July 25th The Grape Picker:
A comedy by Desiree Za

July 26th Poppy Peek-A-Boo:
Children's theater witch magic tricks, puppets

July 27th The Queen Bee: J.L Delaruche, Amy Hech Martin Vole

July 28th Pirates Ahoy!: by Micky Lah with Jenn Miranda Labo, Peter

July 29th The Coffee King:
Musical Comedy wi O'Hara with Donat Huffington, Lara Pi Alex Press

July 30th Lovesick: A come by Nicholas Taup Eugenia, Bernadet Roman

July 31st Basket of Crabs
Financial satire n embarassed Bibi John Grogan Ste

CLUE SIXTEEN: A Singing Duel

The schedule said that on the twenty-fourth of July, at 8:30 P.M., the premiere of the opera *Kidnapped* would take place, starring the famous soprano Arabella Ducoffre. The night before the premiere, a preview took place. It was only open to the most respected opera fans and journalists. The lights dimmed, the crowd was silent, the conductor lifted his baton, and the overture began. The star took the stage and began to sing a beautiful, dramatic solo.

The solo was certainly dramatic, but it was definitely not beautiful! The singer's voice was so terrible, the conductor put down his baton and plugged his ears. The audience was horrified. Until, suddenly, Arabella came onstage to confront her double. The audience was confused: two identical stars? Was this a joke?

"Get off the stage, you fake!" the real Arabella cried.

"But . . . who . . . how . . . how?" stammered the woman. She started to back away and looked around frantically for a hiding place.

"Helen, if I catch you, you'll be sorry!" Arabella called out. The public applauded—the real Arabella was back!

Helen couldn't hide for much longer, or could she? Unfortunately for her, the three detectives had snuck into the show and just spotted her!

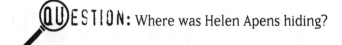 **QUESTION:** Where was Helen Apens hiding?

CLUE SEVENTEEN: Robinson Sulks

At a signal from the theater director, the curtain fell. While Tony ordered Helen Apens to leave her hiding place in the clamshell at stage right, the director tried to calm the audience: "Ladies and gentlemen! Music lovers! Because of a little mix-up, which I beg you to forgive, the show will begin again in a few minutes. Please be patient. I promise that you will soon hear the inimitable voice of our beloved Arabella Ducoffre."

Just then, Arabella's beautiful voice rang out through the theater. She sang, "The sorrowful fate of a princess betrayed, what a mortal menace haunts my days. I remain attached to my one love true, I will be faithful, I promise you." The violins sobbed, the oboes murmured, the bass drum boomed, and the audience took out their handkerchief.

The imposter, named Jessica Ceyrol, was caught. She was an aspiring singer, but her career was over even before it had a chance to start. And Helen Apens joined Jeffre Lincoln in prison.

"And Robinson?" Lily asked David while the audience celebrated Arabella's performance.

"It's true," said Josh. "He was a little neglected during this investigation."

"He's mad at me for ignoring him," David admitted. "He bit me and then flew away!"

"I see him," Josh said. "Take out the peanuts, David. It's time to apologize."

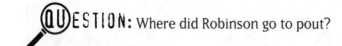 **QUESTION:** Where did Robinson go to pout?

CLUE ONE: An Uncommon Grandfather

"Robinson is so sneaky!" Lily said, remembering the night at the Hillsdale Opera House a few weeks ago. "He hid himself under a top hat on the shelf backstage."

It was a beautiful autumn afternoon, and the friends were on a train to Seaside where Josh's grandparents lived. They were invited to spend a week vacationing in the fresh air, Robinson included. The train slowed down as it approached the little train station. From the window, Josh could already see Castor and Pollux, his grandfather's horses, attached to a cart, but his grandfather was nowhere to be seen.

The detectives gathered their suitcases and waited for Josh's grandfather on the train platform. Josh sighed. "That's my grandfather for you: loveable, but always a little bit forgetful. Let's hope he didn't forget us altogether!"

"Do you think the horses came to get us by themselves?" Lily joked.

"They're capable of it," Josh laughed. "They know the way and they love to watch the trains."

"What does your grandfather look like?" David asked. "It will be easier to find him in the crowd if we all work together."

"That's easy," Josh smiled. "My grandfather never wears a tie, and he hates hats even though he's practically bald. He doesn't have a beard or a mustache, and he doesn't smoke a pipe. It shouldn't be too hard to find him."

"I see him!" Lily jumped up and down excitedly.

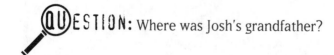 **QUESTION:** Where was Josh's grandfather?

CLUE TWO: An Abandoned Beach

"Josh!" called the jovial man wearing round glasses, who was talking to a man in polka dot pants. "Over here, my boy! Don't you recognize your grandfather?"

He hugged his grandson. Josh introduced his friends.

"Welcome, children! I'm thrilled to have the famous detective trio here in the quiet little town of Seaside. However, if you're hoping to find any mysteries to solve, you'll be disappointed. There haven't been any pirates or smugglers here for centuries. But the ocean air gives us healthy pink cheeks, and you all look like you could use a little color. Go ahead, jump in the back of the cart! Grandma is waiting at home with lunch, and you must be getting hungry. Go ahead, Josh, you're driving!"

Grandfather passed Josh the reins, while David and Lily watched admiringly. Twenty minutes later, everyone was sitting together in the farm's big kitchen, where Josh's grandmother, Regina, served them warm roasted chicken just out of the oven.

"And for dessert," she said. "I made—"

"Your famous chocolate cake!" Josh finished excitedly. "I can't wait!"

Later that afternoon, stuffed with chicken and chocolate cake, the friends walked down to the beach. It was practically deserted at that time of year. The cold wind whipped their faces as they played tag, threw rocks into the ocean, and collected shells.

"No, I must be dreaming!" cried David suddenly. "Look what I found! This is straight out of an adventure novel!"

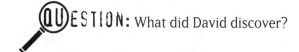 **QUESTION:** What did David discover?

CLUE THREE: Message in a Bottle

Underneath the root of an old, dead tree on the beach, there was a green bottle hidden in the shade. It was corked and carefully sealed with wax.

"A message in a bottle!" yelled Lily. "Should we open it?"

"It looks like the bottles of cider they used to make around here," Josh told the group.

"I want to open it!" Lily started to pry out the old crumbling cork, and with the help of a nearby stick, she finally got it out. Inside the bottle was a rolled-up piece of paper tied with string. Lily took it out, unrolled the yellowed paper, and read the barely visible message written on it:

"Large reward for rescuing me from this place. J.P., Octopus Island, August 1964."

David turned to Josh. "Does Octopus Island mean anything to you?"

"I think it used to be a prison."

The three friends asked a fisherman where the island was. He told them with a mysterious smile and a mischievous gleam in his eye: "Look where the wind blows and you will find what you seek. If not, ask the seagulls."

Lily and David looked at each other, confused. Josh understood completely.

QUESTION: How could the detectives tell which way the wind was blowing?

CLUE FOUR: The Tale of the Octopus

Josh explained to David and Lily what his grandfather had taught him one windy day while they watched seagulls on the beach.

"Seagulls always position themselves with their beaks toward the wind. That way their bodies create the least resistance to the wind."

"Very good, my boy!" said the fisherman, who had followed them to the port. "I'm heading to Octopus Island myself. If you'd like, I'll take you there. Here's my boat, the Water Nymph. Climb in, it's perfectly safe! And allow me to introduce myself: I'm Ivan Addison."

As they headed toward the island, Addison told the detectives the story of the infamous pirate after whom the island was named.

"He was called Captain Octopus because no boat ever escaped him. He pillaged all of the ships he encountered and then sank them after killing the whole crew. The island was his headquarters. It was where he hid all of his treasures hundreds of years ago. He was eventually captured, tried, and beheaded."

The boat pulled into the port on Octopus Island. "If you come back to the dock at six o'clock, I'll bring you back to Seaside."

The friends thanked Addison and jumped out of the boat. They had only three hours to solve the mystery of the message in the bottle. There wasn't a minute to lose!

"Wait!" said Lily, who was looking at the boats in the harbor. "Only one boat here is from Seaside. Can you guess which one?"

QUESTION: What is the name of the boat that Lily recognized?

CLUE FIVE: False Alarm

"I recognized the boat by the flag with a diamond on it," said Lily. "But I don't remember its name. Can you read it?"

Josh squinted at the boat and started to laugh. "That boat's name is Mail Boat. I don't think the boat that brings the mail to the island is very suspicious, do you?"

"I guess you're right," Lily admitted. "Okay, where should we start investigating?"

"How about we start with the name of the person who wrote that message forty years ago," David proposed. "All we have is a set of initials: J.P. We don't know if it's a man or a woman, or if they're dead or alive."

"We don't even know if this person is actually living on the island," Josh added.

"Well, we know the person is not in prison," said Lily. "It's been closed for twenty-five years. Ivan Addison told me it was made into a museum. Should we start there?"

"I think we should go to the cemetery and see if there's a tombstone that has a name with the initials J.P. That seems easiest to me," David said.

Octopus Island's cemetery was located next to the town's church. Josh, David, and Lily scoured the cemetery for any sign of J.P.'s tombstone. After a while, David stopped in front of a cracked tombstone. It all seemed to match the information from the bottle! He called Lily and Josh over to show them what he had found.

 **QUESTION:** Which tombstone did he want to show them?

CLUE SIX: A Sea Dog on Land

While Robinson made friends with two ravens perched in a nearby willow tree, the friends studied the tombstone of Jack Potter, deceased on November 7, 1964.

"Three months after the message in the bottle was written," said Lily. "That's strange. He must not have been very old."

"Maybe he was in a car accident," said Josh, without thinking.

"While he was in prison?" David asked. "You'll have to explain that one to me."

"If you're talking about Jack Potter," said an old lady with a watering can in her hand who happened to be passing by, "he died from a heart attack, the poor man, the night before he was supposed to be released from prison. Are you family?"

The detectives didn't know how to answer her. "Um . . . well . . . I mean . . . not really . . . we just wanted to know . . ." they stammered.

"Well, if you'd like to know more about Jack Potter, ask George Austin, the oldest sailor on the island. You'll find him at the Foghorn. He smokes a white pipe."

The three friends walked to the restaurant the old lady described. It was very crowded, and every table was full.

"He must not be here," said Lily.

"You're wrong," replied Josh. "I see him."

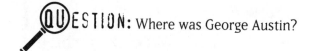

QUESTION: Where was George Austin?

CLUE SEVEN: Followed?

George Austin was sitting with his fellow fishermen at the back of the Foghorn. He seemed to be a talkative and friendly man, so the detectives introduced themselves.

"Three apple ciders for these young folks, please, Miss," he said to the waitress after Josh, David, and Lily explained the mystery to him. "What should I tell you about Jack Potter? That we worked on the same trawler? That he wanted to get rich so he could buy his own boat? That he dreamed of finding a treasure—"

"What treasure? Captain Octopus's treasure?" interrupted David.

"Unfortunately, I don't know anything about that. He was a little bit odd, that Jack. What's more, he had a bad history of stealing. Someone on the island accused him of stealing the treasure that he kept in a box buried under his apple tree. Some neighbor recognized Jack snooping around there one night, and he was thrown in jail. The police never found any evidence of a crime in his house, though. He was about to be released when he died suddenly, carrying the truth with him to the grave."

"What about the owner of the treasure?" Lily wanted to know.

"He died as well, a little while after Jack."

The friends noticed that it was already six o'clock, so they thanked George Austin and hurried to meet Addison.

The following morning, Josh, David, and Lily returned to Octopus Island, this time to visit the old prison. On the walk to the prison, Lily turned around suddenly.

"I have a feeling someone is following us," she murmured.

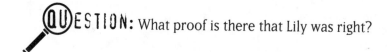

QUESTION: What proof is there that Lily was right?

CLUE EIGHT: Towers!

Someone was following the detectives!

In a gap between the stones of the wall they had just passed, they saw a head quickly disappear. Was it a man or a woman? They couldn't tell from so far away. They decided to pretend like they hadn't seen anything and continue walking. When they came upon a boulder, they hid behind it and waited. Other than the distant bleating of goats and the cries of seagulls, it was silent. Josh poked his head out.

"No one. The coast is clear. Let's keep going."

They followed a path that led them straight to Siren's Rock, the highest point on the island. The view was amazing. The houses, the trees, the lighthouses, and the boats all looked like little toys from so high up.

"Remember," David reminded his friends. "George told us that the prison was in a tower."

"Uh-oh," said Lily. "There must be at least twelve towers down there!"

"You're forgetting what else he said," Josh remarked. "He said that the tower is northeast from Siren's Rock. It should be easy to find with our compass. We'll be there in no time."

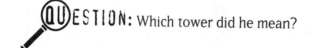 **QUESTION:** Which tower did he mean?

CLUE NINE: Shadowy Souvenirs

Ten minutes later, the detectives arrived at a white tower standing next to a little bridge by the ocean.

The sky darkened. It was windy and dark clouds filled the sky. The detectives heard a crack of thunder, and the first drops of rain started to fall. The three friends ran for shelter in the tower. The tower was deserted except for the tower guard who was reading his newspaper by the light of a storm lamp. When the friends explained that they were there to investigate the prison, the guard grumpily left his post and took them to the foot of a long flight of stairs. He told them the history of the prison:

"Built on the command of Edward Harrison in 1669, the first prisoner of the tower was Harrison's neighbor, Charles Paul, who refused to grant Harrison fishing rights in the surrounding ocean, and also the hand of his beautiful daughter, Eleanor, in marriage. Eleanor avenged her father's imprisonment by burning all of Harrison's boats. Until it closed, the prison housed many infamous men and women, who left their marks on the tower walls. If you climb up the stairs, you'll see."

Though they were afraid, the detectives climbed up the creaking staircase to the top. It was dark, but a flash of lightning lit up the room long enough for the detectives to see the notes and scribbles that covered the wall.

"So many people were imprisoned here!" David exclaimed. "We should find out if Jack Potter wrote his name somewhere."

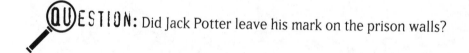

QUESTION: Did Jack Potter leave his mark on the prison walls?

CLUE TEN: Signs and Swans

To the left of the window, below a drawing of an octopus, the detectives found Jack Potter's initials. Next to them was a strange symbol. The symbol looked like a circle with an X through it. While Lily copied it onto a scrap of paper, David hoisted himself up to the window and looked out. "It's a long way to the ocean from here, at least sixty feet," David noted. "There's no way Jack Potter could have escaped without someone's help. He would have needed a saw, a piece of rope, and a boat waiting below."

"Which explains why he would put a message in a bottle promising a large reward to anyone willing to come help," David added.

Lily interrupted. "But if he promised a reward, he must have had some way to pay it."

"Are you thinking of the treasure he stole?" Josh asked.

"Yeah. Maybe he hid it, or gave it to someone for safekeeping."

The detectives asked the tower guard if Jack Potter had any friends or family. "Not that I know of," he said. "Well, no one but his cousin, Felicity Potter. I believe she lives in Swan Cottage."

Swan Cottage? What an odd address! Luckily, Lily remembered that Octopus Island had no street names or house numbers; instead, each house had a different drawing or symbol over its door. All they had to do was look for the swan. Josh spotted it first.

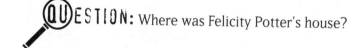

QUESTION: Where was Felicity Potter's house?

The
Golden Duckling
Restaurant

CLUE ELEVEN: A Strong Wind

The three detectives crossed the square, where a fountain bubbled cheerfully. They passed in front of the Black Deer House and walked down the alley separating it from Swan Cottage. Josh, David, and Lily climbed the stairs and rang the doorbell: once, twice, then three times. No answer.

"Maybe she's not home, or maybe she can't hear us," suggested David.

Josh was determined to find out if Felicity was home before they gave up. He noticed that on the windowsill to the right of the door there was a sad, dying plant. Had Felicity gone on a trip? But that wouldn't explain who was taking care of the cat sleeping peacefully on the chair inside. The old grandfather clock Josh spied through the window still kept perfect time. Who had wound it, if not Felicity?

Suddenly, the detectives heard a loud noise coming from the house that almost made Josh fall over in fright. It was a whistling noise that continued to get louder and louder.

"Felicity Potter is definitely at home," David declared. "I can prove it."

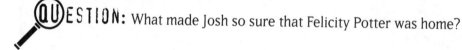

QUESTION: What made Josh so sure that Felicity Potter was home?

CLUE TWELVE: Everyone Has a Little Secret

Josh heard the whistle of the boiling teakettle, and watched as an older woman walked into the kitchen, removed the kettle from the stove, and poured the boiling water into a teapot. Josh knocked on the window and waved. The woman turned around. A few seconds later, she opened the door and let Josh, David, and Lily inside.

"I heard you ring the bell," she told them. "But I was nervous because I live alone. With everything you hear on the radio . . . people taking advantage of the elderly . . . well, you can understand my fear! Sit down and tell me what brought you here."

The detectives decided to tell the truth. They told Felicity about finding the bottle with her cousin's message rolled up inside, and about researching his past. Strangely, Felicity didn't seem surprised that they were there. It was almost as if she had been expecting them. Lily was suspicious. Who had clued her in? Ivan Addison? Possibly. Perhaps the person following them yesterday afternoon was this harmless lady?

"That's a very touching story," said Felicity with a grim face. "I went to visit my poor cousin while he was in prison and I always thought he was hiding something from me, but I never knew what."

"A symbol, maybe?" asked David, referring to the carving they'd seen on the prison wall. Lily kicked David in the shins under the table: She had just spotted a clue in Felicity's living room.

"What symbol?" Felicity asked, leaning forward.

"Um . . . a symbol . . . of affection," Lily answered vaguely.

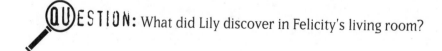 **QUESTION:** What did Lily discover in Felicity's living room?

J.P.
1964

CLUE THIRTEEN: A Mysterious Message

Just then, the telephone rang. "Will you children please excuse me?" Felicity asked.

As soon as Felicity left the room, Lily pointed to the model ship displayed over the armoire and whispered, "That flag has the same symbol that Jack Potter carved into the prison cell!"

David climbed onto a chair, pulled the flag off the base, and found a folded piece of paper. He took the paper out and carefully unfolded it—it was a map of the island, drawn on the same weathered, yellowed paper as the message in the bottle! "M treasure, I send you kisses from behind these bars," David read.

Suddenly, Felicity came back into the room. Furious, she grabbed David's wrist and snatched the paper from his hand. "You little sneak!" she yelled. "How dare you touch the boat my cousin made for me in prison? The one I was told to guard with my life! Get out of here, you brats!"

The detectives felt ashamed for touching Felicity's prized possession, but they had discovered an important clue there. They returned to Josh's grandfather's house and called Tony and Frank, who agreed to come to Seaside later that night. Once they arrived, Tony, Frank, the detectives, and Robinson set off for Octopus Island on a boat they chartered. On shore, they noticed a strange hooded figure lurking near the ruins of an old fort. The shadowy figure tiptoed along the cliffs toward the fort with an old gas lantern to light the way. Suddenly, the figure mysteriously disappeared in darkness.

"Look over there," Josh whispered. "Felicity Potter gave herself away."

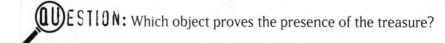 **QUESTION:** Which object proves the presence of the treasure?

CLUE FOURTEEN: An Illuminating Discovery

The group quickly ran toward the lantern that Felicity Potter had left outside of the fort. David blew the flame out.

"I bet Felicity doesn't need a lantern, because she knows the way through the fo by heart," he said. "And she knows where to find the hidden treasure her cousin left he Let's go!"

With David leading the way, the group quietly approached the old fort. They circled it without making a sound, looking for clues and evidence left behind. Behind th weather-beaten bars of a window, Lily saw someone lurking.

"Now we need to find the buried treasure!" David said excitedly.

Just then, Robinson flew off of David's shoulder, where he had been resting, squawked loudly, and swooped down at Felicity Potter who was just leaving the fort, wrapped in a big cape. She hurried away from the fort and across a worn and creaky bridge, accidentally dropping something in her escape from the cockatoo.

"Help!" she cried as she ran away. "Save me from this evil bird!"

Robinson was the first to spot the object that Felicity dropped, and he flew over to it.

"The treasure!" David exclaimed after noticing the leather bag that Robinson w hovering over. "I think we've finally found it!"

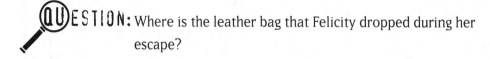 **QUESTION:** Where is the leather bag that Felicity dropped during her escape?

CLUE FIFTEEN: The Golden Octopus

By the instructions left on the note hidden in the ship, Felicity Potter had found a leather bag in a crack in the wall of the fort. She fled as quickly as she could after uncovering the treasure, but Robinson swooped down on her and startled her so much that she dropped the leather bag. The bag rolled a few feet until it stopped underneath small stone bridge, which is where the detectives found the treasure. Everyone crowde around Lily as she opened the leather sack. When she pulled out a giant golden octopu with tentacles made of sapphires, diamonds, emeralds, and rubies, everyone gasped: It was beautiful! The octopus was also incredibly valuable, because it was Captain Octopus's only stolen treasure that had never been found.

The next morning, Josh, David, and Lily proudly turned the treasure over to the island's museum, and it quickly became its most popular attraction. Felicity Potter felt terrible about scolding the three detectives, she also donated Jack's three-masted ship. After all, it was what started the treasure hunt!

This exciting adventure wiped the three detectives out, so Lily, Josh, and David spent the rest of the week relaxing at Josh's grandparents' house, eating plenty of homemade chocolate cake, and hunting for seashells on the beach. Josh taught David and Lily how to drive his grandfather's cart, and they drove all around Seaside with Castor and Pollux. Josh, David, and Lily planned to take a break from their lives as the best detectives in Hillsdale, but only for now! Who knows what other exciting mysterie were in store for them?